This Ladybird Book belongs to:

SOPHIE
DAniel
William

This Ladybird retelling
by
Joan Stimson

Ladybird books are widely available, but in case of
difficulty may be ordered by post or telephone from:

Ladybird Books – Cash Sales Department
Littlegate Road Paignton Devon TQ3 3BE
Telephone 01803 554761

A catalogue record for this book is available
from the British Library

Published by Ladybird Books Ltd Loughborough Leicestershire UK
Ladybird Books Inc Auburn Maine 04210 USA

FAVOURITE TALES

The Magic Porridge Pot

illustrated
by
MIKE GORDON

based on a traditional folk tale

Once upon a time, there was a little girl who lived with her widowed mother. They were very poor, and one day they had nothing left to eat at all.

The little girl was so hungry that she ran into the woods and began to cry.

"Whatever is the matter?" asked a kind voice.

The kind voice belonged to an old woman. When she heard how hungry the little girl was, she gave her a magic cooking pot.

"Just say the words, 'Cook, little pot, cook!'" she explained, "and it will give you lovely, hot porridge.

"But once the porridge is cooked, you must say, 'Stop, little pot, stop!'"

The little girl spoke to the pot right away. "Cook, little pot, cook!" she said, and to her surprise, it began to bubble!

The porridge smelled wonderful. As soon as it was cooked, the little girl said, "Stop, little pot, stop!"

Then she ate up every last bit!

The little girl ran all the way home.
She showed her mother the magic
cooking pot and told her what the old
woman had said.

Her mother was delighted.

"All our troubles are over," she cried.

And she was right. Because, whenever the little girl and her mother were hungry, all they had to say was, "Cook, little pot, cook!"

Each time, the magic pot would cook them some lovely, hot porridge.

The little girl and her mother could hardly believe how lucky they were.

One day the little girl went out for a walk. While she was away, her mother felt hungry, so she picked up the magic pot.

"Cook, little pot, cook!" she said, and the pot set to work. The mother was soon so busy eating that she forgot to tell the pot to stop!

On and on cooked the pot. Soon the porridge began to spill over the top.

As soon as the mother saw what was happening, she knew that she must tell the pot to stop cooking.

But she had forgotten the words!

On and on cooked the magic pot. First the porridge covered the kitchen table. Then it spread across the floor. Soon the *whole house* was full of porridge.

The porridge spilled into the street and filled all the other houses. Then it began to ooze along other streets.

And still the magic pot went on cooking!

By now the town was beginning to *drown* in porridge. The people started to panic. They ran out of their porridge-filled houses and into the porridge-filled streets.

"Help!" cried the mother. "I must stop the magic cooking pot, but I can't remember the words."

"Help!" cried the townspeople. "Soon the whole *world* will be filled with porridge!"

Just as the porridge reached the last house in the town, the little girl came back from her walk. She could hardly believe her eyes.

"*Please* tell the magic pot to stop making porridge," begged her mother.

The little girl took hold of the magic pot and said sternly, "Stop, little pot, STOP!"

And, at last, the magic pot stopped cooking porridge.

The whole town breathed a sigh of relief. It hadn't drowned in porridge after all.

But, if ever you visit there, be prepared… for porridge, porridge and *more porridge*!